T0209195

Naomi
A Child Forgotten

Barbara H. Clark

BALBOA.
PRESS
A DIVISION OF HAY HOUSE

Scripture taken from the King James Version of the Bible

Balboa Press books may be ordered through booksellers or by contacting:

Balboa Press
A Division of Hay House
1663 Liberty Drive
Bloomington, IN 47403
www.balboapress.com
1 (877) 407-4847

Because of the dynamic nature of the Internet, any web addresses or
links contained in this book may have changed since publication and
may no longer be valid. The views expressed in this work are solely those
of the author and do not necessarily reflect the views of the publisher,
and the publisher hereby disclaims any responsibility for them.

The author of this book does not dispense medical advice or prescribe the use
of any technique as a form of treatment for physical, emotional, or medical
problems without the advice of a physician, either directly or indirectly. The
intent of the author is only to offer information of a general nature to help
you in your quest for emotional and spiritual well-being. In the event you use
any of the information in this book for yourself, which is your constitutional
right, the author and the publisher assume no responsibility for your actions.

Any people depicted in stock imagery provided by Getty Images are
models, and such images are being used for illustrative purposes only.
Certain stock imagery © Getty Images.

Print information available on the last page.

ISBN: 978-1-9822-1256-8 (sc)
ISBN: 978-1-9822-1257-5 (e)

Balboa Press rev. date: 10/20/2018

Naomi A Child Forgotten

Naomi suffered abusive relationships during her younger days she has written this book to help inspire and encourage others who might be going through similar difficulties.

Difference Types of Abuse:

1. Physical Abuse
2. Mental Abuse or Emotional Abuse
3. Sexual Abuse
4. Child Abuse
5. Bullying

Each one of these abuses affects an individual in different ways I will explain how each one plays their part in an individual's life.

Physical Abuse can include any bodily harm to another person signs of physical abuse.

- Hitting
- Punching

- Slapping
- Kicking

Mental or Emotional Abuse is when someone tries to control the mind of their family member.

- Such as insulting that person or calling them names
- Making one feel bad about themselves
- Degradation

Sexual Abuse is not really about sex but about one wanting to have power and control over that individual. Making their partner perform in any sex without their consent.

- Forcibly hurting that person while having sex
- Forcing a person to have sex with others against their will

Child Abuse includes sexual or mistreatment of a child.

- Slapping
- Hitting
- Kicking
- Beating
- Biting
- Pinching

Bullying is the aggressive behavior of other children that make one feel like they have power over that child, which is why they pick on certain ones and sometimes it can be a group of children picking on two or three.

- Name calling
- Ridicule a child
- Taking from them
- Tearing up their stuff

The effects that abuse can cause

- High Blood Pressure
- Bruises
- Black Eyes
- Burns, and cuts

Who are the abusers?

A person who has experienced abuse in their life in the past, see another person difference.

They are:

- Controlling
- Bad temper
- Unpredictable

Statistics

The experts say that four girls and one in six boys have been victims of sexual abuse by the time they reach their eighteen birthdays. Close to 60,000 American children are sexual abuse every year. Other sexual abuse includes one and three women (36%) of them have been raped, stalked, or beaten by their intimate partner. One in five women in the United States reported raped while one in seventy-one men have a claim to have been violated. Over half of the females who report being assaulted by their husband or partner.

An average of 72% of these victims has Post-traumatic stress disorder.

Some 71% have depression, between 40% and 75% have anxiety disorders. On the average, about 7 million children experience domestic violence every year.

The abuser can be a loved one, a boyfriend, a husband, wife, parent, grandparent, a sibling, or another relative. It could even be a coach or your school teacher, or a family friend. It is impossible to tell who the abusers are they are ordinary people just like anyone else. (https://www.better health).

Naomi's Story

Naomi has regained the life that her heavenly father meant for her to live. She often visits churches to worship God with other believer worshiping God bring joy, and peace to her life. Naomi has dedicated her life to living for God and doing whatever she can to help others that are in need.

Naomi knows firsthand what it's like to not have a relationship with your mother to be abused by Mother, Father, and family members raised in a home without love. One thing she wants to share with others is that there is help for their situation they don't have to keep on suffering any longer. They can find that help in Jesus that is where Naomi discovered her deliverance in accepting Jesus as her Lord and Savior. She is not telling anyone to make that decision that is entirely up to that person, but it will be one of the most significant decisions anyone could ever make.

Naomi doesn't regret the change she made it has set her free from thinking evil thoughts that no one cared about her or the hurt and pain she endured, the rejection from family members. The attempts to comment suicide along with all the problems that came from being physical, sexual, mental and emotional abuse she thought that suicide was the answer to all her struggles. When she began to read her bible, she starts to see thing differently.

When Jesus went to Calvary to give his life for the whole world He carried all suffering to the cross with Him; He suffered rejection, emotional pain, abuse, and torment. Naomi was not only abused by family members but, after she got married, she suffered mistreatment from her husband. Jesus said it finished over two thousand years ago when He died for Humankind and the sins of the world. God has taken away all the hardships Naomi experienced in her early years she has forgiven all. She was looking for love and attention in all the wrong places but never receive it. That is the problem today a lot of people are looking for love but looking in the wrong places and doing the wrong things to obtain it. Have you ever heard that song what the world needs now is love sweet love that song still stands clear today? Love is the answer, and it can be found in Jesus Christ because He is love. Therefore, He can do nothing but give love in return.

After Naomi gave her life back to the Lord, she got healed of rheumatoid arthritis she had difficulties walking. Naomi used a walker and sometimes a wheelchair, but God has restored her, and now she can walk without the walker. All the praises belong to God Almighty Naomi is in the best health of her life. There is love, peace, and joy in accepting the Lord as Savior and having a personal relationship with Him. Naomi read a book by the Copelands called Limitless Love the title Go for the Overflow.

"We also have a surer word of prophecy: whereunto ye do well that ye take heed as unto a light that shined in a dark place, until the day dawn, and the day star arises in your heart" 2 Peter 1: 19 KJV.

If you have had a tough time in life, if you feel especially unloved because you've suffered severe mistreatment, it may take some time for the revelation of God's love to break through the darkness of those experiences and shine brightly in your heart.

There might be moments when you think you've grasped the truth of it, only to find the next moment that truth has slipped away.

If so don't be discouraged. Just do what this scripture says and keep taking heed to the word of love. Keep looking up scriptures that tell how much God loves you. Then purposely think and meditate on those verses. Talk about them with other believers. Confess them to yourself.

Saturate yourself in them until your heart gets so full of the truth in them, it overflows and washes away the lies of the devil. That's the real love of Almighty God. (Gloria & Kenneth Copeland)

Naomi went back to school and finished with her GED then went on to a technical college to finished with a certificate to work as a Certified Nurse Assistants. She performed this job for several years. Naomi then went back to college at Colorado Technical University and finished with an Associate Degree in Health continue and complete with her Bachelor's Degree in Health Administration. None of her siblings went to college she was the first one to accomplish this milestone in her family. Along the way, there were times when Naomi wanted to stop and give up, but Naomi kept on pressing and believing that she could do it. With the help of God and reading her Bible with some friends encouraging her that she could do all things through Christ Jesus.

Growing up in the Country

We chased butterflies played with the dogs and the other animals that were on the farm. We didn't have time to get bored there was always something to do feeding the hogs and collecting chicken eggs from the nests when we wouldn't be doing that we were in the field helping our Dad. The smell of the morning dew on the honeysuckle, listening to the birds sing early in the morning, the frogs cloaking first thing in the morning and again at night. There was never a dull moment, the Country back then was a peaceful place to grow up.

My parents didn't have locks on the doors they had latches, the screen doors only had hooks that was easy to remove we slept with the windows up. People can't live like that know someone will break in on you and your family in this day and time we live in now and do you harm.

My life began in the South on a farm; my Dad was a sharecropper. Dad was considered at that time a hired hand. Dad kept the farmer's crops up by cultivating the grounds for planting and harvesting. Once the harvests were ready, Dad would give the ones that were old enough a hoe and teach them how to hoe the grass, weeds, and nut grass out of the peanuts and watermelons. If the wild plant had grown to close in the vines, we had to pull it out with our hands it left blisters.

We had to learn how to pull cotton out of the buds go down the cotton rows with a big wool sack on our back-pulling cotton," that woolsack and the heat from the sun was no match" if you didn't do it right your fingers would bleed the buds were very sharp working on the farm helping our Dad.

I asked my Mom one day where children came from she told me a Midwife delivered me at home. My other sisters and brothers were born the same way that was not the answer, but at the time it was the right one for me.

They called them Midwives back in the day when it was time for my Mom to give birth my Dad would go and pick her up from home sometime a family member would bring her out.

The Midwife would stay with my Mom until it was time for the baby to be born and then she would do what she had to do to get the baby here. All the work that she had to do to deliver that baby she should have been called a Nurse she did the profession. Doctors didn't come out at that time only the Midwives deliver children then.

As time passed, we began to move from one shack to the other the houses we lived in were always run-down shacks, never was good for staying. Dad didn't have a problem with that he never had to pay any rent on any of them, the other good thing about that is he never had to pay for water either. We had a well back then we used kerosene to light the lamps and lanterns no electricity. I remember the time we lived in one old house we could see the stars at night from our bedroom there were holes in the ceiling.

When it rains we put buckets out on the floor to catch the water, there were holes in the walls we would take brown paper bags, newspapers, and sometimes old clothes to stuff in the cracks, the rats were the reason for the holes.

My family have lived in the pasture with the cows fenced in with them, there were big rats in our home they were as big as a puppy. They would come out at night looking for food some time you could spot one running around during the day. The rats tore holes in the flour, sugar, rice, and anything else that they could cut with their teeth.

One night one of my sisters went to bed without washing up after she had eaten she got bitten by a rat. The rat had been nibbling her mouth she was kicking and fighting us why sleeping she through we were messing with her. The next morning, we saw where the rat had been nibbling her face it was swollen and had been bleeding.

During the Christmas Holidays, the farmer would give my Dad a bonus for helping him that year. Dad and Mom would go to town and Christmas shop they would buy all kind of candy, cookies, cakes, fruits and different kind of nuts for the family. That was the most candy, and stuff we ever got was doing the Christmas Holidays back in the day we only got these treats once a year. The children would eat cake, candy, cookie, and fruit all day you could tell we were not used to this much at one time. The other times when we got it was when we had a job and could go to the store and get it ourselves that was not often. There have been times when Dad would take all of us to the warehouse to pick up food because there were times when there was a food shortage. Some commodities were rations as surplus food, and you could only get it from the government warehouse where they gave it out.

During the Winter months, Mom would put all of us in a bed together we would get up at night and get the clean clothes out of the closet and put them on top of our bed so that we could stay warm. Especially during the night when the fire had gone out in the fireplace, all the wood had burned out, and it was cold in there. Back then there weren't any heaters to stay warm by Mom had a potbelly stove that she prepares our food on and a fireplace to keep warm. We didn't have a refrigerator either my Dad would buy big blocks of ice and keep them in an ice box or a cooler then he would put whatever meat he had on the inside with the ice.

During sweet potatoes harvest the family would take the potatoes and lay them in the ashes in the fireplace and roast them they sure were good like that. The children would all hover around the fire trying to stay warm sometime if you stood there too long your legs would start to stinging.

Naomi

One evening, while Dad was out working a tornado came the wind was blowing with torrential force. It was snapping trees blowing debris over the yard trees was being thrown into the air Mom was afraid of severe weather. Mom would gather all of us children around her, and she would be in the middle of us like a mother hen do her little chicks. Then she would tell us not to make a sound, so all we could hear was what was going on outside. However, this one time I went to the door open it and told Mom to come on let's go to the neighbors down the streets. "She grabs me just in time" I could have been caught up in that tornado alone with the rest of the family, but God kept us.

When it was all over we all went outside to see what had happened; it was a lot of damage that had taken place, trees were leaning over some of them broken in half parts missing from the house. Dad had to find somewhere else for us to live the house needed a lot of work done. Back then no one brother to do work on a house that required a lot of repairs done to it by the time you did that you could have built you a house from the ground up. The family moved with what they had left from the tornado. Dad found a home with the help of the farmer that was better than the ones we had lived in before. This house had plenty of shade trees with flowers, and some of them even had fruit growing from them this was a blessing it was a whole lot better than the others houses.

We were not in the pasture with the cows anymore there was a pond behind the house in the backyard not very far from home. I would go down there and fish it became a hobby for me one I enjoyed very much. Mom would get after me for going down there alone one time I went down there and started to throw my pole and hook in the water all a certain I saw something. This thing was something that I had never seen before it was big when I saw it I forgot all about fish, pole and everything I left there running as fast as my legs would carry me with fear in my heart. I never told anyone what I had seen that broke me up from going fishing alone. I overheard my Dad telling Mom one day that alligators were in that pond.

On the weekend my parents would go out on the town to have some fun I guess I might have been around twelve months old at the time. Dad would take me on the inside of the bar it was called Shady Lane he would sit me on the countertop then he would go to the jukebox and find his favorite record to play. Then he would sit and talk with the other men while listening to his favorite record drinking beer. Mom would always stay in the car and wait for us I guess that if she had not been pregnant, she would have gotten out, but she never did afterward Dad would buy some extra beer to take home for him and Mom to drink later.

When I was old enough, I like playing on the outside with my toys in the yard on one occasion while playing on the outside a snake crawl up next to me.

I thought that I could play with the snake to me it was just a big worm. However, it was not I had no idea that my life was in danger at the time the snake could have bitten me, but it did not harm me. The snake crawled right by me and went on its way. By the time it got past my Mom had come to the door to check on me in time to see the snake go on about its business. When she saw it, she was frightened for me she came and got me I said to her I was not afraid of the snake.

I had a little red rocking chair that I treasured very much, when my sister came alone I would share my toys with her I finally had someone to play with me. My sister didn't like to play on the outside she wanted to stay in the house. That didn't stop me from playing with my toys on the outside I still had fun all by myself.

Bullying

Mom started to have children every year I would have a sister or brother until it was eight of us. By this time, I was old enough to start school in the first grade on the weekend I would spend time with my Grandparents. It would be lonely there sent I was the only child there, and I would miss my sibling very much and want to have someone to play with me. So, my Grandparents would let me come home and spend some time with them. After getting there, I would soon be ready to go back to my Grandparents. Things were not that good for me even before my parents moved to the city. I used to get punished for letting a classmate who rode the same school bus as me; she would take my hair bows out of my head and wouldn't give them back. She was the school bus bully if she saw something she wanted she would grab it just so happen that she also ends up in the same classroom as me. This girl was huge, and she would always pick on me I was afraid of her. Mom told me that if I let her take one more thing from me that I would get punished the girl end up taken other stuff from me. My Mom told me that when I got off the bus, I might as well stop by the tree and get her a limb off it because she was gone to beat me for letting this girl take my stuff from me. If the tree limb were not to her satisfaction, she would go outside and get another one. It would be bigger and have knots all over it, and she would beat me with it. I was already afraid because of this girl, and then I had to get a whipping because of her, I would run and hide. Mom would be getting her tree limb. What I did that for she would be talking and breaking tree limbs from the tree and she would say you are only making it worse for yourself? Whatever, she had to do on the inside she would go ahead and do it when it starts to get dark I would come out of my hiding place only to get the worse whipping I had ever grasped. When she finished, I had knots and blisters all over my body, and on top of that, I was bleeding in places. I had to learn how to take my stuff back of fight for it.

Moving from the Country to the City

After my parents moved to the City that is when my life began to take on a whole new outlook. Dad moved us in a Jim Walters Home it was not new because other peoples had stayed in it before us, but to us it was new. A Jim Walter Home was the thing back in the day when your parents moved into one of those you had step up. The house was set up in the bottom of the neighborhood it was the only house there at the time. Later, other people began to have homes built down there, and some even had their home moved to that location. Dad had left the farm the farmer had started to take sick and was not able to carry on the farm, so it ends up with other relatives. Dad got another job working with a peanut company I think he liked that job a whole lot it was in an air condition facility.

Our new home was in walking distance of the school we attend me and my sibling that was school age at the time would walk down past the Church and cross the highway, and there was our school right across the road.

Drop Out of School

I had a school teacher who called me names she told me I would never amount to anything I used to hear that a lot especially from my parents. They would say you good for nothing and stupid no one ever going to want you if you ever get a man he is going to leave you with a house full of children. All I ever heard from my parents was negative words they didn't know any other words except negative. Why did they say those things to me? All my teachers were not like that one I had one that was nice to me. She had a significant influence on me, and I wanted to be just like her. I started telling people when I finish school I'm going to college and major in teaching. I desired to make a better life for myself than the environment I was raised up. I had even plain out how many children I was going to have and what kind of house I wanted to live in it was going to be a beautiful future for my husband and me. This teacher had a significant influence on me I quit trying to comment suicide I started to feel good about myself and what I could accomplish in life. It's hard when you are on a high like that and then falls flat on your face look like I was stuck. Later, I dropped out of high school the school principal took me to court because I was not old enough to drop out right then. When my birthday came around, I quit all my dreams gone. The next time I was influenced by a cousin, who didn't go to school because she had dropped out and was running around in the streets making out like she was having so much fun. Which I learned the hard way that it was just a lie she was pretending she was not having fun. At the time my parents didn't care if I went to school or not long as I got a job and helped them pay bills. After getting the job, I find out that this is not what I want to do so I decided to go back to school. I went back it was not easy for me because I was embarrassed, and the principle and his wife wanted me to start in a grade lower than what I left. I didn't want to do that, so I end up going back home and finding a job, so I could help my parents pay the bills.

Grandparents

My Grandparents moved to the city too they were near to where we lived it was not as close as the school was to us, but it was within walking distance. Now I could spend as much time with them that I wanted to that was every day that I got the chance. My sibling didn't spend that much time with our Grandparent as I did they would buy me stuff and give me money whenever I came around them. My sibling became jealous of me they could have gotten the same treatment if they had spent time with them. My sibling began to dislike me I didn't know at the time why all of them would want to get into fights with me, I had no idea or what was going on they start to treat me as if I was an outcast. They began to take my toys and tear them up, and all I tried to do was to share what I had they wanted nothing to do with me. I began to stay with my Grandparents as much as my parents would let me because there were times when my parents would not let me spend time with them. My Grandparents on my mother's side never cared anything for me they tag me as being the black sheep of the family.

Barbara H. Clark

When I was at home, my parents would make me clean up after the other children. They would make me rake the yards, wash the clothes, and do the dishes. They would not make them do anything they were old enough to help do chores around the house but was never told to do anything. I knew then that my parents were mistreating me they began to make fun of me and call me ugly names. It hurt me to be made fun of by my parents I didn't know what to do I did a lot of crying and feeling sorry for myself. Then one day my parents left home to go somewhere and when they left me, and my sibling got into a fight. My brother went into my parents' bedroom and got my Dad's rifle and point it at me and he said:" I will kill you!" Why? Did he want to kill me I was his oldest sister but at the time that didn't matter to any of them. I was considered the black sheep of the family I had learned from an early age that I had to protect myself because no one else was going to do it for me. I have always been a quiet nature person easy to get along with anyone not wanting to harm anyone, but that is not permanently the case sometimes other people want to do you harm regardless.

Abusive Father

My Dad became abusive toward me after moving to the city; my Dad changed a lot he would start at my Mom, he would come home from work upset about something and take it out on her. If Mom said anything he would beat her, we would go and hide to keep from seeing him beaten on our Mom. Sometimes we would go on the outside so that we couldn't hear or, see him hitting on her. Dad would get his rifle and start shooting it when he did my Mom would run out the door, and all of us would be right behind her running to the neighbors down the streets. Almighty God was with my family no harm ever came to us from the rifle. There were other times he would arrive home on his lunch break on Friday and sit in the car until he had finished eaten and then he would come in the house and get clean up and go back to work. The children would stand in the door and peak at Dad why he sat in the car and ate we didn't have anything in the house to eat. The only time we would get anything would be later in the evening when his shift was over then he would take my Mom, and they would go and buy groceries.

After a while he started to take his anger out on me he would get off work and go hang out with men that were younger than he was. Dad would go with his young friends and smoke weed and drink with them. Then later he would come home high and find the least little thing to get upset about if you looked at him that made him angry if you got in the way that made him angry. One incident Dad came home, and out of nowhere Dad just began to beat me for no reason I guess he figures he didn't need a reason to beat up on me. Mom and my sibling did nothing or said anything. I think they feared that he might get them next, so, they stayed to themselves. He was like a crazy man at times that needed someone to beat up on I don't know why I had to be that person.

Dad would bully people on his job and at home when his young guy friends would come around. He used to tell his friends that he had a daughter that he wanted to marry out of the house that might be while a lot of them came around. He tried several times to get men from his job to talk to me, and that would be what they would tell me.

One evening why standing around in the yard Dad came home messed up on weed and who knows what else. When he got there, I was standing out in the yard and all a certain he picked up a brick and threw it after me if it had not been for my sister Clara pulling me out of the way I would have gotten hit with that brick. Clara got struck on the leg with it he had already been beaten on me before he threw the brick Clara took me down to my Aunt's house, and she asked what was going on. We tried to explain as best we could we couldn't make any sense out of the whole thing it all happen so fast. My aunt made me, and my sister stays at her house until he went into the house and fell asleep then he would get up as nothing had happened. When the Grandchildren came alone, Mom and Dad mistreated them too. My Dad had his pick and choice of which one he would pick on these were young children, they had not started school yet, he would kick them and even slap them in the face. They would beat them with whatever they found it made no difference. I had children at that time, and I left them with my parents because I had nowhere else to leave them at the time, I didn't have a choice. As time pass Dad starts to get sick, and the doctors had to start cutting on him. They remove a part of one of his legs because of diabetes later after that he had gangrene to sit up in one of his feet then they had to end up cutting some of his toes off. My Dad realizes his mistakes, and how he had mistreated his wife and children he calls for all of us children, and he said I want to ask all of you to forgive me for the way I used to mistreat you 'all. I don't know how the others may have felt, but I told him I had forgiven him a long time ago it was no problem for me to forgive him. One of my sisters said she would never forgive him even after he passed Clara said she wouldn't do it, but the time came when she didn't have a choice. She had to forgive because her time had come on her deathbed she asked God to forgive her, and she also had to forgive it was not for his release but hers.

Sometime later I found out that my Granddad had lost his life that was hard for me because I was always close to my Grandparents. He got ran over by the tractor that he was working on trying to change a flat tire. When my Granddad died I was not allowed to go to his funeral I was never told why. The same thing happened when my Grandmother passed they let me pick out her casket and her clothes that she was to be put away in and that was it. I was never giving a reason as to why I could not attend their funeral. I don't have a clue.

They were trying to spare my feeling, but it didn't help me any at all, I was hurting for a long time I think it would have helped me to deal with their death better if I could have attended their funeral.

Mother / Daughter relationship

Every daughter should have a relationship with her mother that is an essential part of a girl's life is to be able to communicate with her mother. A girl should feel good about talking with her mother about personal problems and other things that are going on in her life. The daughter should feel good about sharing relevant information with her mother. Her mother should be someone she can confide in about anything. A daughter love to share things with her mother and she has a sense of protection when she is with her mother. She should have a knowing that there is nothing her mother will keep from her especially if it going to better her in her life later when she is older. She should not have to go to an outsider for information when she has a Mother. So often it is not like that the time when I needed my mother the most she wouldn't give me the time of day. She would tell me to go on and leave her alone she had other things to do and didn't have time. If a mother doesn't show any interest in her daughter when she tries to talk to her she will miss out on a lot of things that are a concern to her daughter; The daughter will find someone else to confound in even though she would much rather share with her mother.

There was a change going on in my body that I didn't understand; I end up asking a friend or family member who was the same age as me at the time. What is happening to me, I enquired? My friend or a family member would tell me what to expect and what I needed to do. I was reluctant to ask another adult because I didn't know what to expect from them. Mom never knew when I started my cycle until one day I came home, and my clothes were messed up. Then she starts to explain to me how to take care of myself so that wouldn't happen again. They finally begin to teach Health Education in School about the female reproductive cycle, and that is when I learned what I needed to know about a woman going through change.

My mother wasn't there for me in a lot of ways especially when it came to telling me about the facts of life. I never had any animosity against my mother I have even heard others say it was the way she was raise reason she didn't tell you the stuff you needed to know. Somehow or another I wish she had put all that stuff behind her, but she didn't I needed my mother so much to tell me thing, but she was never available for me. I needed and wanted a relationship with her, but she only pushed me away. I have healed from the rejection of those days, and I have forgiven my mother because my life had to go on and I couldn't keep holding on to that and be free. My Mom is no longer living before she left this world Mom had a lot of issues on the inside of her that she needed to release. God gave her the time to release it, and I hope with all my heart that she did.

Rape

I had my eyes on a young man who I liked and wanted to get to know him, so I asked my sister girlfriend to tell him that I wanted to talk to him. She did so he came by one day, and we began to talk to each other nothing serious just casual talk. At that time, I had noticed that his eyes were always red and often wonder what was going on with him but never asked. The reason for his eyes being red each time he came to see me was because he was on a high. I find out later that he was already involved with another girl they were having problems. If I had known I wouldn't have kept talking to him, it would have been no problem for me to stop the friendship. We kept on talking in an informal way it was nothing serious between us; we would sit on his car and pass the time in front of my parent's house my Mom would watch me like a hawk. Every move we made she was somewhere peeking at us. I did the most talking he was a great listener, and I enjoyed someone listens to me for a chance at least I thought he was paying attention. I didn't find out about the other girl until much later, they had broken up, so I began to consider him as being my special friend. One weekend during the afternoon he asked me if I wanted to ride around in the neighborhood I thought that would be nice. At that time that is what the young people did on the weekend especially on Sundays ride around in the community with their special friends. One Sunday he asked me to go riding with him not thinking that anything would come from it I decided to go riding with him. Little did I know this time he had other plans he took me around the blocks a few times and then to the country he headed. Then he told me after we had got so far out there that if I didn't do what he wanted. I would have to walk back home because he was not going to bring me back home and he was going to leave me out there. His parents didn't stay too far from where he had taken me, but I didn't know his parents or anyone else who stayed out there. Charles drove off the highway onto a path that leads to a field it was getting late in the evening. Charles stopped the car and made me get into the back seat of the car, as I did he made me lay down and pull off my pants then he began to tear my undies off. Charles then forced himself on me, proceed to rape me I couldn't stop him none could I bear the pain. It hurt so bad the ripping of my flesh was just so much pain I beg, "stop, please stop" I tried to get free from him, but I was so small compared to his weigh on me that made him force himself even more. The more I tried to get free the more he would have his way. He would not stop until he finished what he was doing. Afterward, there was blood all over the backseat of the car all over him and me. His words I didn't know you were a" virgin" like it made any difference to him he said I thought you had had sex before. I don't know how he thought that because he was the first guy that I had started to talk to it didn't matter to me what he said. All I wanted to do was to get as far away from him as I could. And I never wanted to see him again I pull up what was left of my clothes back on as fast as I could and made my way back to the front seat of the car in so much pain I could hardly walk.

On the way back home, I couldn't even look at him after what he had done to me I was nervous and scared wondering what was going to happen when I got home. What would I tell my mother if she asked me where I had been? I sat next to the car door that if it had a crack in it and came open, I would have been on the highway. I couldn't even think straight Charles couldn't get me home fast enough I had the nasties feeling on my body, and the stink was awful I felt so dirty and nasty. Finally, I was back home I didn't say anything to him I just got out the car and went into the house I wonder where my Mom was and if she was peeking at me then if she was she didn't say anything to me. I went straight to the bathroom and began to run water in the tube I scrub and scrub my body until it hurt trying to get that nasty feeling off me. I hide my clothes because they were messed up, and later I throw them away. I had begun to trust this man, and I thought he was my special friend, and this is the way he showed me what he thought of the friendship I never wanted to see him again. After that, I didn't see him for a long time until the news got out that I was pregnant. Mom never told me what to expect when someone rapes you what does that supposed to be like or how do you deal with that? Now I start to experience more change with my body instead of her telling me what was going on she told me I went and did what she said for me not to do. Mom never asked me what happen she assume that I went and laid up with a man. Now she is telling me I got to marry this man because I'm pregnant from him, she acts like this was the only answer for me and I didn't have any say so in the matter. I never told him I was pregnant; he got the news from the streets that I was pregnant then he comes by wanting to talk to me, at first, I didn't want to talk to him. Eventually, I listen to what he had to say he asked me if I wanted to marry him because my parents had told him we had to get married. My answer to him I'm not going to marry anyone especially not you. My life and I did have a choice in the matter, and I refused to go through with it, others thought I should have taken the offer. Other girls my age was getting pregnant, and their mothers had booked them to the clinic to get abortions. During the time I find out that I was pregnant until I lost the baby I never went to the clinic for a checkup. I stayed sick the whole time; I would lay around and feel bad until one day my Mom gave me some pills for the sickness. I was inexperienced she gave me four tiny pills and told me to take all of them, so I did. She even said to me that if I didn't swallow the pills that she would know I didn't think anything of what Mom was saying because I figure she was trying to help me feel better.

About a week later after taking the pills, I began to have pain in my stomach and side I had to go to the bathroom and sit on the toilet. I sat there for a while and finally I felt the need to past something it hurt badly. Then I felt the need to push with all the strength I had, and I kept on pushing until I passed something. When I did I heard something fall into the toilet I realized I had lost the baby that I was carrying I was afraid to look in the commode I couldn't. I couldn't tell anyone what had happened. I got up from the toilet with my back to it and flush it never looking back. I went into my bedroom and cleaned myself up, and that is where I stayed. Wondering what I have done after that happen, I started being sick again this time I was in the hospital for Kidney Infection. People were coming to visit me and asking me where my baby is the only thing I could tell them was I didn't have a baby I had a kidney infection. I didn't know what else to say to them after being released from the hospital the Doctor talk to my Mom I don't know what he told her, but she never told me anything. I still had to deal with the fact that I had lost my child it took me a long time to get to where it didn't bother me as much. At the time I had no idea what type of pills those was that Mom gave to me until I asked a friend about them. This friend she knew about stuff like this because she had experienced it she told me that my Mom had given me quine pills to get rid of my child. She even showed me the same pills that I had taken, so she knew what had happened. I had never received anything like that I thought my Mom was trying to help me feel better. My Mom's intention was to get rid of my child, and she did I wouldn't go around other people that much afraid of what they would say. However, it was hard for me to deal with it continue with me for a while, little by little I began to get over it but never the idea that I had lost a child by the hands of my Mom. I guess she thought she was doing what was right in her eyes; I remember her talking about hearing a baby crying I wonder if it was my child. As the years went by a neighbor told us that the people who stayed in the house earlier had killed a child there I believe others had died there too.

The Tent Crusade

The small rural area we lived in there was a lot of killing going on in our town if they were not killing each other they were fighting and stabbing each other. Every weekend you would hear of someone get killed or getting hurt up at the juke. One man got murdered at the juke under the building is where they found his body he was trying to hide, but the bullets found him. It was a welcome change when we heard that a Tent Crusade was coming to our hometown to bring change and help the people to do better.

The Tent Crusade came to our hometown; everyone was looking forward to it the people had heard so much about it from surrounding towns. They had heard about people getting healed in the meeting. After the Tent Meeting got to us, it was a welcome change for many, but not all, people were being healed right there in my hometown. There was a young girl who had worn braces on her feet's and couldn't walk without them they went all the way up her legs. The Man of God called the prayer line after he finished preaching the Word of God and asked if anybody wanted their healing. She wanted her healing, so she got into the prayer line, and she receives her healing. That girl went down that ramp after The Man of God prayed for her and God healed her right then and there. She pulled them braces off and began to walk around there under that Tent without them praising God for her healing. It was so exciting to see her be free from them braces and everyone was happy and praising God for what he had done. That young lady has been free from those braces now for around forty-eight years. That wasn't the only miracle that took place that night there were others. People got healed from blindness The Man of God would spit in their eyes, and they began to see. But it was still other that was skeptical they kept saying aren't anything to that, he just shocking people with the belt he wore around his waist that was a microphone. One woman who was called up had a limb that was shorter than the other one, there were some people there who didn't believe that God was healing the people, so he asked them to come up closer, so they could see what was going on.

He had the woman to sit in a chair and then he had two of the Tent Crusade workers to hold her legs up, and you could tell that one leg was shorter than the other one. The Man of God then called for one of the people from the audience to come and look at it and make sure it was the way they said, and he agreed that one leg was shorter than the other. He then asked him to stay there as he prayed for the woman right there as the preacher prayed for her something began to happen, he said to the man what do you see? He began to shout it" growing it's growing." The man saw with his own eyes that God had healed that lady's foot he went back to his seat telling others what he had just seen. There were problems with the Law people was calling saying the music was too loud and some came out and made fun of the meeting. The devil and his demons were lurking around the Tent during the services The Man of God had to stop and cast out demons from people. The Man of God kept right on preaching the word of God, and people who wanted healing got their healing. People who wanted to give their life to the Lord was born again. The preacher was preaching Heaven high and Hell hot he made the altar call for people who wanted to give their life to the Lord and didn't want to spend Eternity in Hell.

After hearing the word people came running to the altar to repent of their sins and make a change in their life at the time I was a preteen but, I also knew that I didn't want to go to hell.

The last night of the Tent Crusade he had his secretary to get the names of the ones who wanted to join the Church. I was one of them that participated at the time the preacher hadn't sit up a Church we were attending another one until he sat up his Church. Some went back into their old ways, and habits others held on to their commitment to God and what they had learned in the Crusade Meeting. Afterward, the preacher sat up a Church in our hometown it was in the year 1971, the people who meant business for God now had their own Church Home. Even though I was a preteen at the time, I missed that Crusade and that Pastor I would meet them again during the Sundays that we were scheduled to be at the Head Quarters Church. When we all met up there, it was just like being under the tent, and I got to meet the other Saints we enjoyed each other's company. I got to meet his wife and their children such a loving family. All of us that had joined up with the Church had to get baptized; we got baptized in the river the song leader was singing an old familiar song take me to the water when I got in that water something happens to me. The Pastor took me under, and I came up with that same feeling I had experience under the Tent I was no longer the same. I didn't understand what had happened, but I did know that I was no longer the same for a while I didn't want to do things that I knew was not right. The Pastor had preached out other Church's he had place Pastors over them; they were scheduled to come in at the Head Quarter Church, on the same Sundays that we were scheduled. I and my sisters, cousins, and the older Saints got to meet our other sisters and brothers in Christ that we had not become acquainted. After a while we started missing Church a lot because there were difficulties get to the Church, we finally quit going it always stayed with me somehow, I knew that God would open a way for me to return. Things did slow up for a while in our little town, why the tent was there after it left a lot of the people went back to their old ways a great deal of them gave their lives to God but didn't keep the commitment.

Backslide from the Church

After suffering mental, physical, emotional, and sexual abuse I had nowhere else to turn, I was a teenager that had suffered so much until I didn't think anyone cared. I would go into my secret place where I would talk to myself through began to come to me some were good, and others were not. One was to start by reading the word of God and see what he thinks of me, so I read. I began to study my bible, and through those pages, I read about how God loves me.

For God so loved the world that he gave his only begotten Son, that whosoever believeth in him should not perish, but have eternal life John 3:16 KJV

I start going back to Church dedicated my life back to the Lord I made new Christian Friends I enjoyed going to Church. Start participating in Church Activities in the Church my life began to change for the better. I was giving a position to teach young people Sunday School Class even though some of my students were about two years younger than me. I liked going to the Church to participate. I would pick up paper off the yard sometimes they needed raking I would do it if the Pastor's drinking utensil required cleaning I was glad to do it whatever I could find around there I made myself available.

I was staying in my place, and God was blessing me I had a checking and savings account all my bills paid, and I had money in my pocket.

The man I mentioned earlier in this story had found his way back into my life, and I had gotten pregnant with him a second time before I went back to the church. Later, he left me with two children went on his way.

After God had done so much for me this man came over to my home one-night pretending that I meant so much to him I fell for it. I lost all my religion that night on that couch I had plunged back in sin.

First Car

At the time I had no way of getting around to take care of my business, so I asked my Dad to help me get a car. It took a while before he would do it I guess he got tired of me' bugging' him about a car. Dad took me to the car lot it was a used car lot the dealer did his financing we looked at cars to see which one I liked. I saw one that I liked a whole lot I showed the car to him, he kept on looking and said that wouldn't be a good car for me. He showed me the car that he thought I should have it look like the oldest car on the lot it had dents in it and it was rusty. I looked at that car and thought you have got to be kidding me I was looking at a nice clean car you say I need this one. It had dents in it, it was rusty and look like the driver had driven it up against something on the driver's side because it was all dented up. I did not like none did I want this old beat-up car when it was all said and done it was the only car that he would help me get. I had to make payments on the car every month until I paid for it. After that, I never asked my Dad to go car shopping with me again. He figures that since elderly lady drove it, it was a good car, but it was not she had gotten her share of that car.

Barbara H. Clark

I must admit that the car got me to where I needed to go. I went shopping at the grocery store and anywhere else I needed to go. Until Charles took it and gave it to his brother after that, I didn't see the car anymore

Marriage

Some of the same incidents kept recurring in my life as I write this story the reader will be able to understand why I need to get this out in public. Someone might say that has never happened to me, and then there could be others who will say that the same thing happens to me or similar. Understand that things happen to people that sometimes they don't have control over because of the circumstance they might be facing at the time. We all have choices sometimes we don't always make the right decision then we end up living them out or doing some drastic things that we regret later.

I continue to go to Church, but it was not the same I lost the position I had teaching the young people. I couldn't stay in God's presence knowing that what I had done was against the teaching of the Church. I came forward and admitted what I had done I was put on silence by the Church Officials I was not allowed to participate in any activity in the Church. At the time I would have to be in silence for at least three months. After the three months was up you could ask for forgiveness and start over I kept going for a while, and soon I just gave it up. I left the

Church several times I had not grown up in the Body of Christ to the point where I was utterly dependent on God, but God never gave up on me I am thankful that He didn't.

Then I find out I was pregnant again with child number four from this man I didn't know what to do. I went to one of the Ministers of the Church, and I asked her opinion on the matter.

Sarah listens to what I had to say then she began to tell me what she thought I should do about the situation. Sarah replied since you already have children from this man you should go ahead and marry him I went ahead and started making plans for us to get married. All the why thinking that it was the right thing for us to do since he kept end and out of my life for so long.

Charles agreed that we should get married he told his Mom and Dad and I told my Parents we were going to get married we sat the date and decided that we would go to the Court House. My Mom and other family members gave us a reception at my Mom's house when the word got out people began to show up. Charles Mom and his sister and her husband came out, but he was nowhere in sight I got on the phone and called to his home he picked up and I asked him was he coming out to the reception he said he would be there. That was something I should have noticed, but I paid no attention to it other things began to happen.

We got married in front of the Judge she began to perform the marriage I was so unease everything in me was saying no I looked at him and I could tell he had other thoughts too. Neither one of us was happy about it we should have left that Court House, but we didn't try to convince ourselves that this is the right thing to do. We went through with it, and after it was over, I went back to my Parents house and then left for home. Charles went with his friends I didn't see him anymore until sometime later the next day.

When a couple gets married, they spend the first night of their marriage together not with friends or with family members. They want to be together because they love each other and want to spend the rest of their life together. In the long run, you don't get married because you are pregnant or because you have children from him where the love is? Some might say it will come on later we been together for a while it never happens for us. Our marriage was more of a sad occasion than anything there was no happiness involve things were starting out on the wrong note. Charles had a job I worked for a while before my post ended because of lack of work during that time being pregnant and looked to find a job was not easy. However, I would go to the unemployment office and signup for my unemployment checks; it took a while before they began to come in at that time bills started to get behind.

Bill collectors start coming by asking for their money and as soon as I began to get the checks I had to pay bills and catch up statements. Since I was paying my bills, I was hoping that Charles would pay the house bills well he did what he was going to do if it was anything else it didn't get done.

Charles and his Female Friend

Then of all things I find out that he was seeing someone else, he was always going and coming whenever he wanted too. One day I needed a receipt for something I had looked in the house for it but couldn't find it my next thought was to go and examine the car pocket. Low and behold what I saw was not what I was looking for there they were another woman's undies laying up there in the car pocket. I went back in the house and began to question him about what I had just found he began to be in denial about the situation and said that his brother was with his friend and left them there. That was a lie if they were then why was he pushing and hitting on me?

Charles got the undies and left home I don't know when he came back home, I walked the floor, and peak out the windows wondering if he would come back home. Finally, it got to the point where I didn't care if he ever showed up again. I have no idea how long the relationship lasted between him and the other woman.

After our son was born our marriage was still suffering, we needed things for the house I couldn't buy them. My unemployment checks had run out at the time I had to reapply and see if I could draw anything again. My children and I did without a lot of necessities they went without school clothes, school supplies, and shoes. He acts like he didn't care about us if he was getting his needs met. Charles would come home after he had been with his female friend get into bed with me and then take advantage of me. That was just like the first time he raped me it only brought back memories of what had happened so many years ago. Sexual abuse is the same as being raped we were married, but that didn't matter it was still the same. Charles was never intimate with me, and each time he took from me I would get pregnant. One day why riding together he looked me straight in my eyes and dared to say to me I guess every time we do something you are going to get pregnant.

The last time he did that I had a nine-month-old child and was pregnant with twins Charles had begun to hate me because of the pregnancies. It was not my fault I couldn't get pregnant by myself if he weren't forcing himself on me it might not have happened. Charles wouldn't help with the children; we had an old refrigerator that the door had come off the hinges it still worked well, the door just had to have something behind it to hold it up to the fridge. He starts putting a chair behind the door of the refrigerator to keep it up it would stay until someone moved it, in the condition that I was in it would have taken a lot of effort for me to lift the door down. Charles left for work one morning and didn't move the chair from the refrigerator me and my kids we didn't have anything to eat, so I did what I had to do without any help I removed the chair and lifted the door down from the refrigerator. I was hurt and broken I went to my bedroom began to talk to the Lord I asked him why I was living like this my husband didn't care about me.

He didn't love me he never once said I love you, yet I was still there having his babies. When you're married, it's nice to hear your spouse tells you ever so often how much they love you it makes you feel cared for and appreciated. When you live with a person part of your life and never hear that it makes you wonder what is going on I even tried to be loving toward him, he would push me away. After all the pain he had put me through I wanted to make it work being pregnant with twins and carrying around another baby I began to think of ways to abort my kids. I know I was wrong for even thinking that but, I was so miserable and hurt that I thought it would help me somehow. However, I had to go back to God and ask him for forgiveness because I couldn't get rid of them God knew my heart, and he knew that I was hurting. I asked the Lord to see me through these difficult times I didn't know how I was going to make it the way I was living. Charles came home one evening we got into an argument about something, and he began to beat me in my face with his fits my face was all swollen, and my eyes were all red.

My children and I left him that day and went to my parents I was all big with them twins looking like I was gone get sick anytime we stayed there for a while. One morning I got up and got dressed and decide to walk to the mailbox it wasn't that far up the street. As I went up the road, I began to have pain I kept on walking now, and then I would stop and rest I went on and got the mail then I started back. I was having pain off and on went on to the house not long after getting there they had to take me to the emergency room. After we arrived, they took me to the emergency room the Doctor came in and checked me and said that he would have to induce labor. Any woman who ever had to have labor induced no precisely what kind of problems I was having the Doctor got them here I don't remember if they were alive when they came or not. My Mom told me I had, had them and they were going to cremate them, they said the boys weighed about four lbs together I wanted to see them, but couldn't they thought it was best that I didn't see them. They told me they were tiny babies I did get to name my boys.

After leaving the hospital, I went back to my parent's home some of my sisters were still living at the house during this time my husband kept coming by asking me to go back home. I didn't want to go back home to him, but for convenience, I went back with the children.

Drinking Problem

Charles begins to drink more he hung out with younger guys, they would meet up at our house, and he would get with them they would spend the rest of the day together. Later on, during the day after they had had a good time, they would bring him back home. Charles would be so drunk his friends had to carry him into the house. He couldn't stand up they would bring him in the house to the front and leave him there on the couch eventually he would roll over on the floor. That is where Charles stayed until he came to his senses when Charles did he would find his clothes in one pile, and his wallet would be near them. When he looked in his wallet he didn't have any money in it he blames me and says that I had taken his money I didn't have it. The next time it happens he came home like that I took his wallet and looked in it to see if he had anything that time he did, so I got what I wanted out of it since he blames me for taking his money. His friends were robbing him blind they did that after they had got him drunk, it took a while for him to catch on to what was happening. After Charles find out what was happening, he quit hanging with them now and then they would come by for a visit he wouldn't drink with them anymore. Charles still would drink but not with the young guys he would drink alone or with his brothers, he once got drunk and went to sleep under someone's car. The person got in their car to leave and when he started the car up that is what awaken him if he had pulled off or backup he would have got ran over.

Charles Health

Charles health begin to get bad he was a heavy smoker, so he decides to give up smoking little by little Charles gave it up afterward he didn't smoke another cigarette. Then he decides he would give up drinking it took some time, but Charles did it he didn't drink anymore. Even after he had accomplished these milestones we were still having difficulties in our marriage things should have started to change for the better, but it never happens. For some reason or the other, we never could sit down and talk about our marriage and try to work things out. Charles would always talk to his sister Dean, and his brother John before he would speak to me. Whatever was going on with me I had no one to talk to I didn't want to talk about my marriage with any of my relatives, I kept it on the inside and dealt with it as best I could. My children were all growing up I spent a lot of my time with them my oldest was getting ready to finish high school the one next to her was not that far behind her, she would soon be getting ready to finish high school. The younger ones were participating in different activities at school that took my mind off a lot of what was going on at the time I was working it helped too.

New Job

They were getting ready to close that plant down before they did I had found another job it was out of town it paid more, and it was a twelve-hour night shift job. I had no reason not to take the responsibility after all my children can take care of themselves it meant that I would work every other weekend and have every other weekend off and every other three nights and have the other three offs. However, it was going to take some getting used to it was hard work the money was good, but you had to earn every cent of it by the work you put out. After training it was my turn to perform at first, I didn't think I was going to make it I hung on in there going home every morning half sleep under the steering wheel I was determined to make it work. After my trial was over within those three months, I had learned how to master my job and keep up with the machines I was running.

One night I notice this guy who worked in the back watching me he would come in the breakroom every time I would be on my break. He would sit and stare at me then one night he came to my table and introduced himself and asked me if I care if he sat with me I said no and told him my name we began to talk. Pretty soon David starts to show up in my department where I worked trying to speak to me often I would be busy trying to keep my machine running I didn't have time to talk to him. At some point David got around to asking me if he could see me after work I said no he was very persistence another girl I knew had started to work there too so I told him about her and that he should talk to her. David started talking to her, but David always made his way back to me asking the same questions. I said what about the girl I told you about he said he was only interested in her as a friend, but he wanted to know me better than that. I told him I'm married, and I don't want to get into any relationship with another man. David said like it was no surprise to him I'm married too we are having problems in our marriage, so I want to talk to you, I never told him my situation with my Spouse. Thinking about my issues at home and what I had to go to after work I began to have second thoughts about being with him. David wouldn't give up, and I eventually gave in we would meet after work and spend some time together after a while we begin to date. David and I would have some of the best times it was more than what I got at home. I finally find out what it meant for a man to be intimate with a woman in the bedroom after I met David. I was scared by the fact that both of us was married and this was wrong I had a husband to go home to, and he had a wife to go to this had to end. It did but not before I had fallen in love with him it was not easy, but I had to let him go a man had finally come into my life who showed me things could be different than what I had experienced for several years of my married life.

Charles begins to get suspicious I was coming home later than usual, by know it was over it still didn't change our relationship he was still the same didn't do anything different. One day why Charles and I were out, he dared to ride me right by David's home he was on the outside at the time. David was cleaning his yards I guess Charles was trying to prove a point. So, I finally left him moving out of town I start back to date David it lasted for a few months then we broke it off.

The manager of the plant begins to make changes at the facility one of those changes was the company name later he had changes made on the inside. One was the job that I was performing I had to learn how to do a similar profession to the one I had but, this one was very stressful, and it took a lot there was more work to do. The trainer trained me on how to do this job it took a little longer getting used to, but I manage to learn it. This new job took a lot from me I begin to have problems with my wrists, and hands. The nurse on duty told me that I wouldn't be able to keep doing the job for long. On my off days, I start looking for something else to do that wouldn't be as stressful I was in my ninth year of working there before I turn in my resignation. My boss heard that I had to leave the job because of health reason. He didn't want me to go. The supervisor didn't want to see me go he said that if I ever got better, I could come back to my post I left in good standing with that company. After resigning, I went to a College University to become a Register Nurse I went up until the time I started having difficulties with typing during one of my semesters. I talked with my

Barbara H. Clark

administrator and explained to her what was going on, and then I took leave from there I wanted to go back but was still having problems. After leaving the University, I decided that I would draw my unemployment and figure out what I would do next I withdraw my unemployment until it ran out. Now it was time to find a job I went back to college this time a Technical College to get Certified for Nursing Assistance I work as a nursing assistant before, so I decided to go back to it. I got a job as a live-in nurse assistance with a senior man, and his wife my post was to work three days and night taking care of him in their home. I worked with them for a while and started to have problems with my wrists again, so I soon had to quit it got to the point where I couldn't use my hands like I used to, so I had to leave work altogether. Then I started having problems getting around my feet was giving out on me next thing I had to start walking with a walker. At the time I had left my husband because of my relationship with David that had ended I was in my apartment out of town. After my body began to go down, the Doctor said I had rheumatoid arthritis I had been out there for five years after I left Charles once again my husband came for me to return home with him.

Home with Charles

There was not a whole lot I could do except take my medicine and do the best I could for myself, so I end up going back home with him. I stayed in one part of the house, and he remained in the other side and the children that were home at the time had their room. My oldest daughter moved back in she needed somewhere to reside, so I end up back in the bedroom with Charles. Even though he wanted me to move back in he had a woman friend I don't know how long they dated after I return home we never talked about it, and I never asked. We didn't talk about our relationships even though mine had been over a long time ago. Charles just wanted me there because of the children, and grandchildren whatever the reason our marriage was still suffering.

After the children began to move back out I thought surely; we can start over for the better, who was I kidding? Then his brothers and Dad came into the picture he had lost his mother several years before. His Dad became sickly he starts taking care of him, his Dad was living with his oldest brother and one of the younger brothers. They didn't take care of his Dad the way Charles wanted them to, so he decides to care for his father. Charles brothers would come by the house to borrow money, or they wanted him to run errands for them one of the younger brothers intellectual was unstable, so he ends up taking care of him too. Darrien would leave home walking in the heat of the day going somewhere to find something to drink he was an alcoholic. Darrien didn't care how far he had to go to get it some of the guys would beat him up and take his money and leave him in the street drunk. All Charles did go to work and take care of his Dad; then on the weekend, he would spend the day with him riding him around and take him to different places. His father was like a little kid seen things for the first time he had Alzheimer's Disease.

Some weekend he would load my walker on the truck and take me riding I was glad to get out of the house, but when we got to wherever we were going, I couldn't walk into the place sitting long periods I would get stiff and couldn't move my feet. My feet would freeze I wouldn't be able to move one foot before the other he would have to help me back into the truck, so I stayed home a lot.

Charles had enough going on with his brothers most weekend nights one would come up at a different time of the night want him to take them home. After taken one home later that same night another brother would come up want him to take him home. Charles would put up a fuss and sometimes he wouldn't do it; he soon had to put a stop to that. He began to ride around in the County looking for us somewhere else to live he figure if we stayed out in the County it would be too far out for them to walk.

Chemo-Therapy

Charles started being sickly himself he knew what was wrong but didn't get the children, and me together to tell us until much later the Doctor had said to him that he had cancer. Charles Dad pasted he had already started his Chemo- Therapy he kept on working some days Charles would feel good and other days he wouldn't. During his Dad funeral you could tell he was not feeling well he was sick from his Chemo- Therapy but he was there to see his Dad for the last time.

He continues to do things for his brothers until it got where he couldn't do anything more. When Charles came home from work he would go to bed he would lay there until he felt better. Charles still tried to do what he could for them, but it got so severe with him that Charles couldn't do for them what he once did. Charles had been looking at a house in the County and wanted me to see it he took me to see the house it was a lovely house it had a sizeable front the back was small. I liked the front of the house it needed minor work to fix somethings after looking at the house we went back home Charles never said anything about getting the house. Then one day

Charles came home and told me he had paid two months' rent on the house. We were supposed to have moved in the house after the landlord gave him the lease, but I didn't know it until after he had disbursed the second-months rent. What about the work on the house? Charles said that he and the landlord had talked that over and he had agreed that he would have the job done. We moved into the house as was Charles began to get some of the supplies that he would need to start work on the house. Then later Charles told me about signing papers agreeing to buy the house we never talked anything over and came to an agreement together it was always what he decides to do. One evening after Charles had come home from his checkup at the clinic and told me how all his blood work and all the other test they ran on him came back good. The next day it was time to go and take Chemo- Therapy when he got home he was upset because of being sick from it Charles didn't understand that just the other day things were satisfactory, and all his work came back good, but each time he took Chemo it would make him sick. Charles had mentioned a few times that some of the patients that had started out with him was seeing the same Doctor and they had passed on. I told him to try another Doctor out of town he was not feeling well, so he went to bed. Charles would get up after a while and start doing things around the house this time he just stayed in bed. We had only been in that house for about three months when his health began to worsen. Charles was in bed longer than usual It became a concern I went in to check on him I asked him if he was alright he never said anything he just laid there in a stare. Now and then he would look at me and not say anything. His brother John the one next to him came over and wanted to talk to him the only time he came around was when he needed to borrow money. I went to the bedroom and told him that John wanted to talk to him, Charles still laid there without any response. I asked John if he would go in and check on him, he left without so much as even going in the room to see if anything was wrong with his brother. I went back in after his brother left Charles was still the same I told him I was going to call the paramedics. When they got there, they checked his vital signs he was in critical condition they rushed him to the emergency room. After checking him out they moved him to ICU and began to treat him later that night he started to come around that following morning Charles had begun to talk again. It looked like everything was going to be alright then his oldest brother called, him at the hospital about some business, they had together they began to exchange words. On the next day sometimes, early morning he had a relapse the Doctors had to put him in an induced coma and put him on a breathing machine. As he laid there I could only look at him I didn't know what to say to him at the time. Charles was on a breathing machine it took a lot out of me, I was walking with a walker couldn't get around that good. Trying to be there for him was not easy for me, I did what I could travel back and forth to the hospital. After some days I got a call from the hospital asking for the family to come down, the Doctor begins to explain to me that all his organs had begun to shout down. The Doctor said that I had to decide the faith of his life he said that he would never recover, and if Charles did he would be in a vegetable stage, it was not an easy decision to make. We all agreed that the best thing would be to take him off the machines. When they unhooked the machines, he never regains conscious, he died. Now I had to prepare for his burial me, and the children got together and did what we needed to do none of his family members helped us plan his burial in any way. That was a good thing I believe the children wanted to do it themselves. When it came to the business part one of his family members was always there not to help with the business was just there. I believe that family member was trying to find out his business with his insurance on his job. One of the sisters did have some input as to what I should put on his tombstone it could have been different if they had participated in some of the other things that were going on. Most of his friends came around and helped as best they could the people from his job they helped us out in every way possible. The people he worked with at the hospital all knew him and respected him for his work, and loyalty the CEO of the hospital had a family member to speak at his funeral. When it was all over, I went back to the house lonely and alone I didn't know what to expect now that he was gone. I saw some of the work that he had tried to do why he was sick, and it just tore me up. Charles was finally trying to make it where we could begin our life together in our own home all these years I thought we were finally going to have something together. I was wrong just when things looked like they were going to work for us. I started making plans as to how I wanted to fix up the house. My bubble was bust we had been married for thirty-one years not counting the years when we were off and on again. After he passed, I decided to complete the work he had started I had people to come out and work on the house, but soon find out that the house was not going to be ours. The landlord had forged some illegal papers on him, and he had signed them thinking he was buying a house. I had to get a lawyer to get all this information straight out God worked all of it out I didn't have to pay anything. Then the landlord wanted me to stay there for two more months without paying rent and then start back on the third month my lawyer said I could do that if I wanted too. The children that were with me after their father passed didn't want to continue staying there. My daughter had the first room in the house from the back side of the house, and we made it a bedroom for her and her children Shirley told me after her father had passed that she had encounter spirits in that room. She also said that a baby would come in that room and a couple of times someone would put that baby in her arms in bed. When things get started at night, she would get her boys and sit up in the front living room of the house. Shirley didn't want to be back there in that room she didn't want to stay there anymore. After Shirley had told me this, I would get up at night, and there she would be with her boys sitting on the couch, not in bed. My son would leave the house on the weekend with friends and then stay out late; Dan said he had encounter spirits there too whenever he came home. I remember one time I was sitting at the kitchen sink and someone pushes me off my walker on the floor I fell. My children helped me up to get back on the walker, but I never told them that someone had pushed me off it. I had noticed there was a horseshoe over the front door of the house but didn't think anything about it, and in the room, my daughter had something was buried on the outside next to the window. There was also some things hanging in the laundry room I never thought that much about none of it. If these things were going on before my husband died my children never said anything about it until after he had passed. The house was ancient, and something was going on in there. Why sitting in my bedroom one afternoon after he passed I saw something like a vision it was people figures in a gulf of fire. They were screaming and crying some were talking I don't remember what they were saying. I didn't know what I know now about taking authority over evil spirits and casting them out of my house. We decided that we would find us somewhere else to live at the time I had my daughter, and her boys and my son with me they didn't want to live there any longer.

We moved back to town my daughter and, her children along with my son we decide to continue living together after a while I choose to step out on my own. My life began again on my own I had started to get around better because of prayer my pastor prayed for me often. My Doctor told me I should consider having surgery on my ankle. It took a while before I decide that I would go to a specialist and see, what my odds of having surgery on my ankle would be? The specialist said that I was at risk of losing my whole foot and that he had done surgery on other patients and they came out fine. So, I had a lot to consider concerning my health, but I was believing God that I was going to be okay. The Pastor had been praying for me for healing I knew that God was going to heal me. The Doctor took x-rays of my foot and told me what was going on. He said that all the ligament in my ankle had gone the bones had deteriorated he would have to go in there and clean all of that out. Scheduled for outpatient surgery, I was cut several times on my foot and had to stay in the recovery room for a while before they let me go home. I wore a cast for a few months and had to have nurses come by and evaluate me on my progress. I had to use a wheelchair and my walker to get around until my foot got better at the time I rented a two-wheel shooter so that I wouldn't put weight on my foot. Bye and bye things began to get better I started exerting my foot soon it was time to go back to the specialist.

My progress was steadily improving soon the cast came off I have marks from it on my legs, and feet from being cut but I can walk without a walker and a wheelchair I thank God. That was a miracle for me because I could have lost my whole foot.

Tragedy

Tragedy struck my life again

Five months after my husband passed tragedy hit my life yet again this time it was my oldest daughter. She was not living with me but with a guy friend whom she had been living with for several years. Chole and her friend had been having problems with their relationship because of other women. We convince her to leave and move away to start her life over she talks with her younger sister and her husband about moving in with them until she found work and a place to live. Everything was well thought out she started her life over in another part of the state chole had found employment and everything was looking up for her. Soon after Sam began calling her telling her how much he missed her and wanted her to come back to him. At first, she would listen to his calls and go on about her life she had not gotten involved with anyone else at the time, so he kept calling. One day Sam called and convinced Chole that he wanted her to come home with him he was very convincing because without hesitation Chole began packing up getting ready to move back.

When she arrives back in town my husband and I went out to pick her up Chole was all smiles, and she seems happy to be moving back in with Sam. Chole felt like this was the right thing for her to do Chole was in love with Sam and nothing was going to keep her away from him. Chole moved back in with Sam and soon find work again at the facility she had worked with before things seem to be going fine. Then one day after work she began to see a change in her home, she could tell that another woman had been in her home she questions Sam about it he dismissed it. Chole had already begun to have health problems that she never disgust with me or any of the other family members; she had one friend who she would tell everything. I am sure that her best friend knew what was going on. Her best friend never shared anything with Chole's family that she disgusts with her Chole was having a lot of problems with her job as well. She worked on the night shift, and it would be short of help every night the people would not come to work. Chole had to work under a lot of stress and working alone this job required at least two people to do the work. With her health problems and working she manage as best she could early one morning she got up and started to get ready for work something happen Chole never made it out the door.

Chole had a massive heart attract and passed out right there in the front living room of the house. Sam came home and found Chole on the floor unresponsive he called for the paramedics. When they got there, she was pronounced dead on arrival my son got the message from someone that something has happened he was telling me that my daughter was deceased. At first, I didn't believe him because I said to him they just joking with you he said well I'm going by there and see, I had not been long praying and intercede for my children and others in prayer. The Pastor had put individuals on a different schedule to pray at different times of the day. I would always go to my prayer place where I would sit and pray when it was my time. I remember praying precisely for my daughter to make it in the kingdom not knowing that she was leaving this world but, God. After my son gave me the news, I came along sure enough people were all over the place.

My sisters and other's that knew my daughter was there it was a total shock to me I couldn't believe I had lost my daughter. A few months earlier I had lost her father I didn't know what I was going to do and if I would even make it through all of this but God. I remember the last time I spoke with my daughter she came in the room where I was smiling and said" Hi Mom I love you, and I looked at her and said I love you" I still remember that like it was today. I had no idea it would be the last time that I would ever speak to my daughter again I still miss her.

Another tragic was when my Mom and Dad passed both was in the nursing home at the time I went to visit them whenever I could remember I was on a walker at the time and couldn't get around that good. My Dad had Alzheimer at the time he could never recall who I was, but he could remember some of my sisters but not me. Mom, she reminds all of us, and she would tell us if you had not been by in a while she would sit on the porch with the other residents they enjoy each other's company. My Mom had stomach cancer she began to get sick, and her body started to go down fast she soon passed right there in that nursing home. At first, it seems like my Dad didn't know what was happing we told him that Mom had decreased, and did he know it a week later he had to go to the hospital they had found blood on his covers. The Doctor explains what was going on the problem could be treated, but my Dad refuses he didn't want to live anymore, he wouldn't even fight to live he just gave up and passed on. During that time, we had not buried our mother, so we arranged for them to lay to rest together the Mortician made it possible for that to happen. On the fourth month after my daughter had passed, then my parents died it was just so much one person can endure without the help of God.

God kept me sane through it all there were times when I thought I would lose my mind, but I held on to God. I was going to church regularly, and the more I went, the more I was able to cope with my lose it was good to be around people who knew me and showed me, love. I didn't want to be anywhere else since then I had grown to be a mature Christian. I don't have the mindset that I used to have about the church. Now I have the mentality that all I want to do is live for my Lord and Savior and as I live for him, He has given me the mind of Christ. I am a new creation in Christ Jesus.

Therefore, if any man is in Christ, he is a new creature, old things are passed away: behold all things become new 2 Corinthians 5:2 KJV.

When I join the church as a child, I wanted to live for Christ but didn't understand at that time what the Lord wanted from me and how to go about living for him. I went to Church, and I enjoyed going but had not made a commitment to live entirely for the Lord. As I began to get older, I realize that it was more to living for the Lord than I realized at the time. That is why I kept letting this man in and out of my life because I thought that what I wanted at the time could be found in him. But I was fooling myself each time I would go back to the Church never wholly giving myself to God, and each time I would leave because of no reason or another.

Thank God all of that has changed now I am committed to living for the Lord, and it is all I want to do now, I don't have a mind to go back into the world for anything God has become my everything. I am complete in Him everything I need He provide He is my source for every need in my life. I only look to Him to see me through all the problems that I may encounter along the way. Through it all God had never left me even during the times when I was not stable in the Church He was always there for me.

I am getting ready to start a new chapter in my life you can bet that God will be here to see me through it. Even though it will be a new beginning, it will not be without God starting all over again. I had stopped living my life and began to live with my daughter to help her out with her daughter now that time for me here is about to be over. I am looking forward to living my own life once again in my own home and doing the things I like to do. My family is getting ready to move and start over in a different part of the State so, that means I must start over too. God has been good to me, and He has taken care of me all through this time I am grateful to Him for all that He has done for me. There were times when I went through things that I didn't understand why being here and I must say a lot of the time those changes hurt. But as I went on and kept talking to God about the change that I was experiencing at the time God began to let me know why I was undergoing these changes. I was still maturing in the Lord, and I had to endure the move to make me a better person for him. I am stronger than I have ever been because of my faith in God is strong. I don't have a mind to turn from Him in any way. I love the Lord and so thankful that He loves me even more.

Therefore, we are buried with Him by baptism into death, that like as Christ was raised up from the dead by the glory of the Father, even so, we also should walk in the newness of life Romans 6: 4 KJV.

In some way, I hope that this book has encouraged the reader it has given the reader a mind to want to make a change in their life, or it has helped the reader to cope with different abuses in their life. However, it has helped you I hope the most it has enabled you to give your life to Jesus and cast all your cares upon him.

Casting all your care upon Him for He cares for you 1 Peter 5: 7 KJV.

It doesn't matter what you think of yourself or what others have told you that is not what God thinks of you. He loves you for who you are, and it doesn't matter what you have done in your life Jesus still loves you and He want so much to show you just how much he loves you. Give Jesus a chance to love you, even more, it doesn't matter what you have done give Him the opportunity to wrap you in His loving arms and wash away all the fear, the abuse, the hurt, and the pain. If you are willing, you can start a new life in Christ Jesus, and all the old will become new.

Confess today start over with God and let Him be Lord of your life it will be the most significant decision you will ever make concerning your salvation.

Here is a prayer for you will you say it and let go and let God be your Lord and Savior.

That if thou shall confess with thou mouth the Lord Jesus and shall believe in thine heart that God hath raised Him from the dead thou shall be saved. For with the heart man believeth unto righteousness: and with the mouth confession is made unto salvation Romans 10:9-10 KJV. If you made that confession, you are now a new creation in Christ Jesus.

Printed in the United States
By Bookmasters